Here's a Penny

Here's a Penny

Carolyn Haywood

Illustrated by the author

AN ODYSSEY/HARCOURT YOUNG CLASSIC

HARCOURT, INC.

Orlando   Austin   New York   San Diego   Toronto   London www.HarcourtBooks.com

First Odyssey/Harcourt Young Classics edition 2005
First published 1944

Library of Congress Cataloging-in-Publication Data
Haywood, Carolyn, 1898–1990.
Here's a Penny/written and illustrated by Carolyn Haywood.
        p.   cm.
"An Odyssey/Harcourt Young Classic."
Summary: Follows the adventures of six-year-old William, an adopted boy
nicknamed Penny for his copper-colored hair, as he attends a Halloween
party, adopts kittens, and finds an older brother to join his family.
[1. Adoption—Fiction. 2. Family life—Fiction. 3. Brothers—Fiction.
4. Friendship—Fiction.] I. Title: Here is a Penny.   II. Title.
                PZ7.H31496He   2005
              [Fic]—dc22   2004055250
        ISBN 0-15-205227-5   ISBN 0-15-205225-9 (pb)

Text set in Bodoni Classico
Designed by Kaelin Chappell

Printed in the United States of America

                A C E G H F D B
                A C E G H F D B (pb)

To
Caroline Fleischer
My most amusing critic

CONTENTS

Here's a Penny

1

A Brand-New Penny

They called him Penny. His name wasn't Penn or Penrose or Penrod or anything that would make you think of Penny. His real name was William.

Before Penny came to live with his daddy and mother, his daddy had said, "When we get our little boy, let's name him William. Then we can call him Bill."

"Not Billy?" asked Mother.

"Not Billy, nor Willy, nor anything else that ends in *ee*. Just plain Bill," said Daddy.

"Very well!" replied Mother. "Plain Bill it shall be."

But this is how he happened to be called Penny.

Long before Penny arrived, his mother and daddy decided that more than anything else in the world they wanted a little boy.

"A little red-haired boy," his mother used to say.

"With freckles on his nose," Daddy would add. And then Mother and Daddy would look at each other and laugh, just because they had said it so many times.

One day Daddy received a telegram from the head of a big hospital. It said that they had some babies that needed fathers and mothers, so Mother and Daddy got right on the train and went to see the babies.

They looked at the babies, one by one. They were all sweet and cuddly. There was one with black hair and one with hair like a fuzzy peach and there was one with no hair at all.

"Maybe it will be red when he gets it," said Daddy.

"No," replied Mother, "we have to be sure."

And then she spied Penny. He was sound asleep in his little basket. He was the color of a ripe apricot and his head was covered with red gold ringlets.

"Here he is!" whispered Mother. "Here's our little boy!"

Daddy looked at him very carefully. "Is that a freckle on his nose?" he asked.

Mother leaned over and looked at the tiny button of a nose. "I think it will be, by the time he is six," she replied.

Mother picked him up and the sunlight fell on the baby's head.

"My goodness!" said Daddy. "He looks like a brand-new copper penny."

Mother cradled the baby in her arms. He opened his eyes and stretched his mouth into a funny toothless grin. "He's just a dear, precious little penny," she said.

And so they named him William. But they called him Penny.

Now, Penny was six years old with freckles on his nose. He was in the first grade and he loved to go to school.

Patsy, the little girl next door, was in the

first grade, too. Every morning Penny would stand on his toes and lift the brass knocker on Patsy's front door. Then he would hear Patsy's feet pattering, and in a moment she would pop out of the door. Then off to school they tramped.

One morning Penny was full of excitement. "I'm going to get a kitten," he said, the moment Patsy appeared.

"How do you know you are?" asked Patsy.

"My mother said I could get one," replied Penny. "He's going to be a black kitten, with a white nose and white paws."

"How do you know?" asked Patsy.

" 'Cause that's the kind I want," said Penny.

"Well, you can't always get kittens just the way you want 'em," said Patsy. "You have to take 'em the way they come."

"Who said so?" asked Penny.

"My mommy said so," replied Patsy.

"Well, anyway, my kitten's going to be a black kitten, with a white nose and white paws," said Penny.

"I wish I could have a kitten," said Patsy.

"Why don't you get one?" asked Penny.

"My mommy won't let me have one," answered Patsy. "She says she doesn't like cats."

"I'll let you play with mine sometimes," said Penny.

"I want one of my own," said Patsy, kicking a pebble. "I think it's mean of you to get a kitten when I can't have one."

Patsy pouted and there were tears in her eyes. After a while she said, "Well, anyway, I'm my mommy and daddy's real little girl."

Penny didn't know what that had to do with kittens, so he didn't say anything.

Patsy stood still and looked at Penny. "I said, 'I'm my mommy and daddy's real little girl,'" she said in a very loud voice.

Penny just looked at Patsy. He didn't know what he was supposed to say, so he just said, "Uh-huh."

"But you're not your mommy and daddy's real little boy," shouted Patsy.

Penny felt his cheeks grow hot. "I am so Mother and Daddy's real little boy," he replied.

"Oh, no you're not!" cried Patsy. "You're just 'dopted."

"I know I'm 'dopted," said Penny. "My mother told me so. But I'm her real little boy."

"No, you're not," said Patsy. "You can't be. Not really truly."

Penny turned away from Patsy and ran. He wanted to get away from her as fast as he could.

"Not really truly!" cried Patsy. "Not really truly!"

Penny ran faster. Patsy was way behind him now but he could still hear her calling, "Not really truly!"

Penny's little legs flew. His cheeks were hot

and his ears were bright red. He never looked back to see where Patsy was.

When he reached the school, he went right into his classroom. He didn't even stop to say good morning to Miss Roberts, his teacher. He went right to his desk and took out his scrap-book. He made believe that he was very busy. He was really blinking his eyes to keep back the tears. He had to bite his lip to keep it from trembling.

When Patsy came in, Penny didn't look at her. He didn't look at her once all morning. Over and over in his head he could hear her calling, "Not really truly! Not really truly!"

Once Miss Roberts said, "What is the matter with Penny today? He doesn't look very shiny."

Penny didn't look up. He just hammered a nail very hard. He was building a bed for Judy, the big doll that belonged to the first grade. He could hardly wait for school to be over. He wanted to go home to Mother. He wanted her very, very badly.

At last the bell rang. Penny was the first one out of the door. He didn't wait for Patsy. He ran faster and faster and faster all the way home.

The back door was open. Penny dashed in.

Minnie, the cook, was baking cookies. "Land sakes!" she cried. "You look ready to burst."

"Where's Mother?" gasped Penny.

"Upstairs," said Minnie.

Penny stomped up the stairs. "Mother," he called. "Mother, where are you?"

Mother was sitting in the study, darning Daddy's socks. When she saw Penny's face, she dropped the sock. Penny threw himself into his mother's arms. The tears that he had kept back all morning rolled down his cheeks. His mother's arms held him tight. "There, there," she murmured. "Tell Mother what's the matter."

It was a long time before Penny could speak. He just cried and cried and the tears made his

mother's neck all wet. She held him close and said in a very soft voice, "Tell Mother, Penny. Tell Mother what it is."

At last Penny seemed to run out of tears. "Patsy says I'm not your really truly little boy," he gulped.

"Patsy is mistaken," said his mother, wiping his eyes.

"She says when you're 'dopted you can't be really truly," said Penny.

"Nonsense!" said Mother. "There is only one thing that makes a little boy 'really truly.'"

Penny sat up and looked at his mother. His blue eyes were big and round. Teardrops still hung on his eyelashes. "What does, Mother?" he said.

"Why, his mother's love for him," said Mother. "His mother's love for him makes him her really truly little boy."

"And does his daddy's love for him make him his really truly little boy?" asked Penny.

"It certainly does," replied Mother.

Then his mother told him how she and Daddy had talked about him long before he arrived. How they looked for just the little boy they wanted, with red hair and freckles on his nose.

Penny snuggled into his mother's neck. "Did you look at other little boys?" he asked.

"Indeed, yes," said Mother.

"But they didn't suit, did they?" said Penny.

"No. They were very nice," said Mother, "but we waited until we found you. And you were just what we wanted."

"That's the way I'm going to 'dopt my kitten," said Penny. "I'm going to wait until I find a black one with a white nose and white paws. And I'll love him so much that he'll be my really truly kitten."

"Of course," said Mother.

"I guess I'll go get a cookie," said Penny, as he slid off of his mother's lap.

When he reached the door he turned around. "I guess I'll take a cookie over to Patsy," he said. "And I'll tell her she's mistaken."

2

Really Truly

Every time Penny heard of a cat having kittens he would say, "Is there a black one with a white nose and white paws?" Over and over again he received the same answer. "Oh, no! There isn't any black one with a white nose and white paws."

Penny's daddy took him to see so many kittens that Daddy finally said he wouldn't have believed there could be so many kittens in the world. There seemed to be every kind that you could imagine, but no black one with a white nose and white paws.

After a while Daddy began to feel discouraged. But not Penny. After each trip to look at kittens he would say, "You found just 'zactly the little boy you wanted, didn't you, Daddy?"

And Daddy would reply, "Oh, my, yes!"

Then Penny would say, "Well, I'll find my really truly kitten, too." And the next Saturday afternoon Daddy and Penny would go look at another litter of kittens.

One Saturday afternoon Penny and his daddy were walking home from what Daddy called "a kitten hunt." They were walking under some trees when Penny heard a tiny "Mee-u."

Penny looked around to see where the sound came from. He didn't see anything. Then he heard the sound again. "Mee-u."

"Sounds like a kitty," said Penny.

Daddy stopped and looked around. There was the sound again.

"Yes, it does," said Daddy.

Daddy looked up in the tree above him, and there on a branch was a kitten. It was the most

unhappy-looking kitten Daddy had ever seen.
And Daddy had seen a great many kittens. It
was afraid to move and it opened its little
mouth and cried, "Mee-u! Mee-u! Mee-u!"

"Why, there it is! Up in the tree!" said Daddy.
"I'll see if I can get it down."

Daddy stretched out his arms and stood on
his toes. Just as he was about to take the kitten,
the kitten moved away.

"Now, what do you know about that!" said
Daddy.

"He's a silly old kitten, isn't he?" said Penny.

"Mee-u! Mee-u! Mee-u!" cried the kitten.

Daddy looked up at it. "Now see here, pal!" he said to the kitten. "I can't climb the tree. Come over here like a good fellow."

"Mee-u! Mee-u! Mee-u!" cried the kitten and moved still further away.

"Now, what do you know about that!" said Daddy.

"Maybe if you lift me up, I could reach him," said Penny.

"Well, that's an idea," said Daddy. "Let's try it."

Daddy lifted Penny up as high as he could. "Just reach right out for him," said Daddy. "Don't be afraid of him."

Penny reached out and took the kitten off the limb of the tree.

"Have you got him?" asked Daddy.

"Yep!" said Penny. "I've got him."

Daddy set Penny down and they both looked at the kitten.

"He's not very pretty, is he?" said Penny.

"He certainly is not pretty," said Daddy. "In fact, he looks like a scrap of a moth-eaten coat."

"What kind of a kitten do you s'pose he is?" asked Penny.

"I haven't an idea," said Daddy. "But he looks as though his mother had tried to hide him in a pot of mustard."

"What shall we do with him?" asked Penny.

"Oh, just put him down," said Daddy. "He'll find his way home."

Penny put the kitten down. His little legs seemed to wobble. "Mee-u," he said, and he rubbed against Penny's foot.

"I think he likes me," said Penny.

"Well, come along now," said Daddy. "Let's get going."

"Do you think he belongs to anyone?" asked Penny.

"If he does, they certainly don't feed him very much," answered Daddy. "He's as thin as a pin."

Penny stooped down and stroked the kitten. It purred.

"Come along, Penny," said Daddy. "It's getting late."

Penny took hold of his daddy's hand and started for home.

In a few moments Penny looked back. "I wonder where the kitten went," he said. "I don't see him anywhere."

"Mee-u!" said the kitten.

Penny looked down, and there was the kitten right at his feet.

"Oh, there he is!" cried Penny. "Look, Daddy, here he is."

"I see him," said Daddy. "I'm afraid he has decided to come with us."

"Do you think he is going to follow us home?" asked Penny.

"I think he has something like that on his mind," replied Daddy.

"But he's not the kind of kitten I want," said Penny.

"I know that," said Daddy. "But perhaps you are the kind of little boy he wants."

"But he can't be my really truly kitten," said Penny. "Because my really truly kitten is black with a white nose and white paws."

"Oh, I know that," said Daddy.

"Well, what shall I do?" asked Penny.

"We can try saying 'Scat' to him," said Daddy. So Penny and Daddy said "Scat" very hard. The kitten said, "Mee-u," and rubbed against Penny's foot.

"He probably doesn't speak English," said Daddy.

"He looks awful hungry," said Penny. "Maybe

we ought to take him home and give him some milk."

"Maybe so," said Daddy. "One thing is certain. We ought to go home and it looks to me as though the kitten has made up his mind to go wherever we go."

Penny picked up the kitten. It was so thin he could feel all of its tiny bones. The kitten curled up contentedly in Penny's arms.

When they reached home, Penny ran into the house to show the kitten to his mother. "I've got a kitten," he cried.

His mother looked so surprised when she saw the kitten that Penny said, "Oh, he's not my really truly kitten, but he was up in a tree and when we rescued him, he followed us. We had to bring him home to give him something to eat. We couldn't let him starve. I'm not going to keep him."

"I see!" said Mother.

Penny gave the kitten a saucer of milk. He filled up like a little hot-water bottle and looked fatter already. Before Penny went to bed, he put the kitten to bed in a little box in the laundry.

In the middle of the night Penny woke up. He thought of the kitten. *Maybe the kitten is*

lonely in the laundry all by himself, he thought. He wished that he had him upstairs.

Penny got up and tiptoed down the back stairs. When he reached the laundry, the kitten was standing by the laundry door. He looked as though he had been waiting for Penny.

Penny picked him up and carried him upstairs. He climbed into bed and put the kitten on the foot of his bed. Soon they were both fast asleep.

The next day the kitten followed Penny everywhere. By the end of the week Penny loved the kitten just as much as the kitten loved him. Seven days of good food had made the kitten look quite different.

Penny couldn't decide what to name him. Daddy wanted to name him Mustard and Mother thought Yellow Jack would be a good name. But they didn't suit Penny.

The following Saturday Penny's grandaddy came to see him. To Penny's surprise Grandaddy was carrying a basket. When he opened the basket, there was a kitten. A beautiful coal black kitten with a white nose and white paws.

Penny let out a squeal of delight. "Oh, Grandaddy!" he cried. "My really truly kitten!"

Penny picked up the lovely kitten and held him to his cheek. He was soft and silky.

"Mee-u!" came from the floor.

Penny looked down. There was the mustard-colored kitten rubbing against his foot. The kitten looked up at Penny with pleading eyes.

Penny stooped down and picked him up. He held him against his other cheek. The kitten purred.

"What will you do now?" asked Daddy. "You can't have two kittens."

"Why can't I have two kittens?" asked Penny, coaxingly. "I'll take care of them."

"Why, you can't think of a name for one

kitten," said Mother. "How will you ever find names for two kittens?"

Penny's face lit up. "I've got names for them already," he said. "I'll call the yellow one Really and the black one Truly."

3

Patsy's Twins

The day after Truly arrived Penny took his two kittens over to see Patsy. When Patsy saw them, she said, "Oh, Penny! Can I play with them sometimes?"

"Sure, you can play with them," said Penny. "You can play with them this afternoon if you want to. I have to go to town with my mother to get new shoes."

Patsy's eyes shone. "You mean I can keep them all afternoon? Just as though they were mine?" she said.

"Yep!" replied Penny. "But you must take good care of them. Don't let them get lost or hurt."

"Oh, I'll take good care of them," said Patsy.

Penny stroked each kitten and went off to get his new shoes.

For a while Patsy sat in a big chair and held the kittens. She thought it was just like having two tiny babies. *Like having twins,* thought Patsy.

She decided to make believe that they were twin babies.

But if they were babies, thought Patsy, *they would have clothes on.*

With this thought Patsy jumped up. She put the kittens down on the floor and went into her bedroom. Rosalie and Rose Mary, her two dolls, were sitting on her bed, dressed in their best white dresses and bonnets. Rosalie's bonnet was tied under her chin with pink ribbons and Rose Mary's was tied with blue.

Patsy picked up the two dolls and carried them into her playroom. She untied their bonnets and took them off. Then she took off their dresses and their underwear. Then she tucked the dolls into their doll bed and covered them up with a blanket. "Now you take a nice nap," she said to Rosalie and Rose Mary.

Patsy went back to the kittens. She picked up Really. Getting Really into Rose Mary's underwear was quite a struggle. When his back legs were in the right places, his front legs wouldn't go through the armholes. When his front legs were through the armholes his back legs wouldn't fit into the place where Rose Mary's pink legs fitted so nicely. Finally Patsy decided to give up the underwear. She tried Rose Mary's slip. This went over Really's head very nicely and his front legs went through the armholes. Patsy looked at Really admiringly. "Now that's nice," she said. "You look like a baby already."

"Mee-ow!" said Really. Which probably meant, "I don't want to be a baby!"

Patsy picked up Rose Mary's dress. She poked the kitten's head through the neck and his front legs through the sleeves and fastened the button at the back of the neck.

"Oh, you're sweet!" cried Patsy, picking up the bonnet. She decided that blue ribbons would be more becoming to the yellow kitten.

It took some time to put the bonnet on and to tie the ribbons under Really's chin. Really twisted and squirmed and even scratched, but finally Patsy tied the blue bow.

"Oh, you beautiful kitten!" cried Patsy.

Really said, "Mee-ow!" which probably meant, "Phooey!" or something like that.

"Now after I get Truly dressed I'll take you for a nice ride in the coach," said Patsy, as she tucked Really into her doll coach. Really did a good bit of pawing and clawing but he finally

decided to make the best of it and curled up for a snooze.

Patsy proceeded to dress Truly in Rosalie's clothes. Truly made noises that were worse than Really's. He wiggled and squirmed and twisted. Twice he broke away from Patsy but she finally tied the pink ribbons under his chin.

"Now, my beautiful babies," said Patsy, as she tucked the kittens under a pink blanket, "I'll take you for an airing."

Very carefully Patsy took her doll coach down the front stairs and out the front door. Then she looked into the coach to see if the kittens were all right. They were both curled up at the foot of the coach. Really's bonnet had slipped down over one eye. Truly was all tangled up in his white dress and was sticking out of the blankets, tail first.

"Oh, dear!" sighed Patsy. "Such babies!" She picked up Truly and smoothed his dress. She straightened Really's bonnet. Then, pushing the coach before her, she started down the street.

When she reached the corner, Patsy went into the grocery store to spend a penny for some candy. She left her coach standing by the step. Patsy didn't mean to stay in the store so long but she couldn't make up her mind about the candy. She didn't know whether to buy a chocolate marshmallow or a big green gumdrop.

Meanwhile the kittens had wiggled out of the pink blanket and were looking over the side of the coach.

"Mee-u!" said Really. Which probably meant, "Let's get out of this."

"Mee-u!" said Truly. Which surely meant, "You said it, pal!"

And then, racing down the street, came a wirehaired fox terrier. His pink tongue was hanging out and there was a gleam of mischief

in his eyes. He was out for a good time and looking for fun wherever he could find it.

He was just flashing past the doll coach when,
"Wow!"—he spied the kittens. This was just the
kind of fun he had been looking for. He made a
lunge at the coach and over it went. The kittens
flew, bonnets, dresses, ribbons and all.

When Patsy came out of the store, all she saw
were what looked like two white rags, racing up
the street, followed by a wirehaired fox terrier.

Patsy picked up her doll coach and ran as fast
as she could after them.

The kittens ran as fast as their doll-baby
clothes would let them. Really soon lost his bonnet. It landed in a puddle of muddy water.

Truly's bonnet had slipped down so that it

covered his face entirely but he kept on running.

Without knowing it, the kittens ran straight for Penny's house.

Minnie was standing at the back door when the two kittens appeared. At first she thought they were two paper bags, blowing in the wind. But when they blew right past her and into the kitchen, she could hardly believe her eyes.

She banged the kitchen door on the barking fox terrier and hurried to see what it was that had blown in. She looked in the dining room but there was nothing there. She looked in the living room but there was nothing there. Then she climbed the front stairs and went into Penny's room. And there, curled up on the bed, were the two kittens wrapped up in what looked like muddy rags.

Minnie picked them up. She looked at their clothes and at Truly's bonnet, hanging from his neck like a wet bib. "Goodness!" she cried. "Where did you get those clothes? I declare, I never did see kittens dressed up like that before. And just see the mud you got on Penny's bedspread. He's going to whip you when he comes home."

Just then there was a knock on the back door. Minnie went downstairs with a kitten in each arm. When she opened the door, there stood Patsy with her doll coach.

"Oh, Minnie!" she cried. "Are the kittens all right?"

"All right!" exclaimed Minnie. "They're all right, I guess. But they gave me an awful scare, rushing in here like floor rags that had come alive. You take them clothes off those kittens. Don't you know they don't like clothes? They like to run in their skin."

"Not skin, Minnie," said Patsy. "Fur."

"Humph!" said Minnie. "When Penny comes home, he'll 'fur' you. Dressing his kittens up like sissies."

Patsy took the muddy clothes off the kittens. She had picked up Really's bonnet from the puddle. Then she went home, leaving the kittens with Minnie.

When she reached home, she took out her little washtub. She put soap flakes into it and warm water. Then she began to wash the doll clothes.

In a few minutes Penny returned.

"Hi, Patsy!" he cried. "I got my new shoes."

He looked around for the kittens. "Where are Really and Truly?" he asked.

"Oh, they're over at your house," said Patsy.

"Did you have fun playing with them?" asked Penny.

"Oh, yes!" replied Patsy, rubbing the clothes very hard.

"What are you washing?" asked Penny.

"My doll clothes," said Patsy.

"Gee, it's muddy water," said Penny. "How did they get so dirty?"

"A dog chased 'em," said Patsy.

"A dog chased them!" exclaimed Penny.

"It was that nasty old wirehaired fox terrier that lives up the street. He chased 'em."

"You mean he chased Rosalie and Rose Mary!" exclaimed Penny.

"Well," said Patsy, "not 'zactly. But he chased their clothes."

Penny screwed up his face and looked puzzled. "How could he chase their clothes?" he demanded.

"Well, he did," said Patsy. "That's how they got so dirty."

Suddenly Penny's eyes grew very big. "Patsy,"

he said, "did you have those doll clothes on Really and Truly? Did you?"

"Well," said Patsy. "Well, ah . . . well, ah . . . sort of."

Penny frowned and looked very angry. "You did?" he shouted.

Then his face broke into a broad grin. "Gee, I bet they looked funny!" he said.

Then the two children began to laugh and they laughed and laughed and laughed.

4

Another Kitten Hunt

Every day when Penny came home from school he played with his kittens, Really and Truly. One day when he came into the house Really was curled up in the kitten basket, fast asleep. When he heard Penny's footsteps, he opened his eyes and hopped out of the basket. He knew that when Penny arrived it was time to play. The most fun was a ball of newspaper tied to the end of a string.

"Where's Truly?" asked Penny, looking all around.

"Mee-u!" said Really.

Penny went through the rooms on the first floor calling, "Here, Truly, Truly, Truly!" No black kitten appeared.

Penny went upstairs. Really followed him slowly. The steps were high and Really was still very little.

"Mother!" called Penny. "Did you see anything of Truly?"

Mother answered from the bedroom. "Why, no, dear. I haven't seen him this afternoon. I know that Minnie gave them both their dinner at noon."

"Are you sure?" asked Penny.

"Yes, I'm sure," replied Mother. "Because I remember Minnie said that she thought they both ought to grunt instead of mee-u."

"Well, where do you suppose Truly is?" said Penny.

"Did you look on my best sofa pillow?" asked Mother. "That seems to be his favorite spot."

Penny went downstairs to look in the living room again. Really rolled down after him.

Penny looked on the best sofa pillow, but Truly wasn't there. Penny looked under all of the pillows and under the sofa and under all of the chairs. Truly was nowhere to be seen. He went through the house again, calling, "Here, Truly, Truly, Truly! Here, Puss, Puss, Puss!" But there was no black kitten.

"Do you think he could have gone out when Minnie went out?" Penny asked his mother.

"He may have," replied Mother.

Penny went outdoors. He went all around the

house calling, "Here, Truly, Truly, Truly! Here, Kitty, Kitty, Kitty!" There was no answer.

Really stood inside the door, meowing. He wondered what was the matter with Penny. Why didn't he play with him?

Penny went over to Patsy's to see if she had seen Truly. But Patsy hadn't seen him. She joined the search. The two children hunted for the kitten until dinnertime.

At dinner Penny told Daddy that Truly had disappeared.

"Well, now, don't worry about him," said Daddy. "He'll turn up."

"But he's very little," said Penny, "and maybe he doesn't know where he lives or how to get home."

"Oh, yes, he will," said Daddy. "He's a smart kitten. He'll know his way home."

All evening Penny kept opening the front door and then the back door. Each time he would call, "Here, Truly, Truly, Truly! Here, Pussy, Pussy, Pussy!" But when it was time to go to bed Penny only had one kitten to carry upstairs. He felt very sad.

Penny got undressed and washed his face and hands and brushed his teeth. Then he climbed into bed. When Mother came to hear him say his prayers, Penny threw his arms around her neck and cried. "Oh, Mummy!" he sobbed. "I can't lose Truly. I can't lose him. I waited so long for him and now he's gone."

Mother held her little boy close to her breast. "Darling," she said, "who gave Truly to you?"

"Why, you know," said Penny. "Grandaddy gave him to me."

"But what was it that made Grandaddy want to give him to you?" asked Mother. "What makes Daddy and me want to give you things that make you happy?"

"It's 'cause you love me," said Penny, gulping on a sob.

"Exactly," said Mother. "So it was love that really gave you the kitten, wasn't it?"

"Yes," answered Penny.

"And do you remember what you learned in Sunday school last Sunday?" asked Mother.

"Yes," said Penny. "It was 'God is Love.'"

"That's right," said Mother. "Now the love that gave Truly to you is taking care of Truly."

"And will bring Truly back to me again?" asked Penny.

"I'm sure of it," said Mother, as she kissed her little boy.

Then Penny said his prayer. When he finished, he said, "Mother, I said thank you to Grandaddy for Truly, but I didn't say thank you to God."

"Well, you can say it now," said Mother. "It's never too late to say thank you to anyone."

Penny closed his eyes and said, "Thank you, God, for Truly. And for Really, too. Mother, will you lie down beside me until I go to sleep?"

Mother lay down beside Penny. He snuggled up close to her. Soon he was fast asleep.

In the middle of the night he woke up. He thought someone had called him. Penny sat up. The full moon was shining in his window. It made the room very light. Then he thought he heard something that sounded like a very faint "Mee-u."

He sat very still and listened. There was the sound again. It seemed far away. He couldn't tell whether the sound came from outside of the house or inside.

Penny got out of bed. He went to the window. "Mee-u," he heard. He was sure now that it was Truly. But where was he?

Penny leaned out of the window. In a few moments he heard the sound again. "Mee-u." It seemed to come from overhead.

Outside of Penny's window there was a big tree. Penny wondered whether Truly was up in the tree. He listened for the sound again. In a moment he heard "Mee-u." Penny was sure then that the sound didn't come from the tree. He was certain it came from the roof.

Penny tiptoed down the back stairs. He unlocked the back door and ran around the house to the big tree. He had climbed the tree many times. Now he would climb up to the roof and rescue Truly.

Penny started up. Higher and higher he went. He had never been up as high as the roof before. He had always been a little bit afraid to go that high. But he didn't think about being afraid now. All he thought of was that his precious kitten had to be rescued.

At last he reached the roof. The moon was so bright it lit up the roof almost as well as a flashlight. Penny could hear Truly crying, but he couldn't see him. He listened closely. Then he heard him again. The sound seemed to come from one of the rain pipes.

Very carefully Penny crawled over to the rain pipe. He looked. What did he see but a white spot and two round yellow eyes! It was Truly. He was stuck in the rain pipe. Penny could just poke his little hand down to lift him out. Penny hugged him very tight. "How did you ever get up here, Truly?" he whispered. Truly rubbed his head against Penny and said, "Mee-u."

Penny began to think about getting down off the roof. Now that he had to carry Truly it wasn't as easy as it had been to come up. In fact, Penny couldn't even crawl over to the tree. To crawl he had to hold on with both hands. But now one arm had to hold Truly.

Penny sat on the edge of the roof with his legs hanging over. He wondered what he would do next.

At last he thought of something. He stuck Truly back in the rain pipe. "Now you just stay there a minute," he said.

Penny proceeded to get out of his pajamas. It wasn't easy but he finally got them off. Then he tied one leg in a knot and then the other. Then he tied each sleeve in a knot. Finally he lifted Truly out of the rain pipe. He put him inside of his pajamas. It was just like putting him into a

hammock. Then Penny tied the legs of his pajamas together and the sleeves together and hung them around his neck. Now he knew that Truly would be safe.

With both hands free, Penny crawled over to the big tree. He climbed down very slowly. He didn't want to hurt Truly. At last he reached the ground.

He ran into the house and up the back stairs. No one had heard him. He took his pajamas from around his neck and lifted Truly out. Then Penny tried to unfasten the knots in the legs and sleeves of his pajamas but he couldn't budge them. Finally he threw them on his chair, picked up Truly, and climbed into bed. Soon he was fast asleep again.

In the morning when he woke up he found his mother leaning over him. He wondered why Mother looked so surprised.

"Penny!" she cried. "What happened to you?"

"What's the matter?" asked Penny.

Mother pulled the covers down. What she saw made her gasp.

"Why, you're black!" she cried. "Black from head to foot! How did you get so filthy dirty?"

"Oh! I don't know," said Penny. "Am I dirty?"

"Dirty!" exclaimed Mother. "I've never seen anything so dirty."

"Oh!" cried Penny. "I guess all that dirt came off the roof."

"Off the roof!" said Mother. "Penny, what are you talking about?"

"Why, I had to go up on the roof to rescue Truly," said Penny. "He was stuck in the rain pipe, Mummy."

"Oh, Penny!" cried Mother. "You didn't go up on the roof!"

"Yes, I did, Mother," replied Penny. "Truly was up there."

"But why didn't you call Daddy?" asked Mother.

"Oh, Daddy couldn't have gotten him, Mother," said Penny. "Daddy's hand wouldn't have been little enough to get down the rain pipe."

5

Chocolate and the
Queen of Hearts

Every year on Penny's birthday his Aunt Mildred sent him a toy animal. When he was a year old, she sent him a white rabbit with pink eyes and long pink ears. His name was Pinky. When he was two, he received a black woolly lamb called Baa. On his third birthday a brown monkey arrived. Penny named him Little Fellow. When he was four, Aunt Mildred sent him a tawny lion with a big furry ruff around his neck and a long tail with a tassel on the end. To Aunt Mildred's great surprise Penny named him Mildred. The following year she sent him a black-and-white penguin. Penny named the penguin Waffles because he had just tasted waffles for the first time.

But on his sixth birthday Aunt Mildred sent the toy animal Penny was to love best. It was a dark-brown bear. As soon as Penny lifted him out of the box he decided to name him Chocolate. Chocolate had big round ears that stood out on each side of his head and a hard brown nose that looked like an acorn. Penny said it was just the nose for getting into honey.

When Patsy saw Chocolate she thought he was the loveliest thing she had ever seen. She came over to Penny's house every evening before she went to bed, just to give Chocolate a great big hug.

Finally Penny's mother wrote to Aunt Mildred and asked her if she could get another Chocolate.

After several days the big box arrived. Penny and Patsy were playing in Penny's room when Penny's mother carried it in. "What's in the box, Mother?" asked Penny.

"It's a package for Patsy," said Mother.

"It is!" cried Patsy.

Penny's mother put the box on a chair. "Here, Patsy," she said, "you open it."

Patsy's eyes were round with wonder as she untied the package.

"Oh, I know what it is! I know what it is!" cried Penny, hopping up and down on one foot.

"Now, Penny, don't tell," said Mother.

Penny's eyes were dancing in his head because Mother had told him about the bear for Patsy.

When Patsy looked into the box and saw the brown bear she could hardly believe her eyes.

"Oh!" she gasped, as she lifted him out of the tissue paper. "Another Chocolate!"

Then she hugged him very tight and looked up at Penny's mother. "A Chocolate for me?" she asked.

"Yes, Patsy. Your very own Chocolate," said Penny's mother.

Penny was jumping all around the room now, singing out, "I knew it! I knew it! I knew it! I knew it all the time."

"Can I take him home with me?" asked Patsy.

"Of course," said Penny's mother. "He has come to live with you."

"Oh, thank you," whispered Patsy. "I'll take him home right now and show him to Mommy."

When Halloween drew near, Penny and Patsy were invited to a Halloween party at Tommy Robbins's house. The children had never been to a Halloween party before and they could hardly wait for the day to come.

"I know what I'm going to wear to the Halloween party," said Patsy one morning on the way to school.

"So do I," said Penny. "But I'm not going to tell."

"I'm not going to tell, either," said Patsy. "It's a secret. You'll be surprised, all right."

"Well, you'll be surprised, too," said Penny.

One day, when Penny was playing with Patsy, Patsy sent him up to her room to get a game. Penny looked all around but he couldn't find it.

"Patsy!" he called down the stairs. "I can't find it."

"Look on the floor of the closet," Patsy called back.

Penny opened the closet door. There on the floor lay the game. He stooped down to pick it up. As he did so, something fell and hit him right on the head. To Penny's surprise it was a gold crown. Penny picked it up. Then he stretched up on his tiptoes and hung the crown

on a hook. Looking up, he spied a fluffy white dress with bright red hearts sewn all over it.

Penny picked up the game and closed the door. He chuckled to himself. He had seen Patsy's Halloween costume. He decided not to say anything about it. After all, he hadn't been snooping. Patsy had told him to look in the closet. And the crown had hit him right on the head.

The Halloween party was to be Friday evening. When the day arrived, Penny and Patsy ran all the way home from school.

"Mommy says I can put on my costume and come over to your house this afternoon," said Patsy.

"That's fine! I'll put mine on, too," said Penny. "Oh, boy! Will you be surprised!"

"You'll be surprised, too," said Patsy.

"Bet I won't be," said Penny, grinning.

"Oh, yes, you will be," said Patsy, as she left Penny.

Penny ran into the house and upstairs, shouting, "Mummy! I'm home, Mummy!"

Mother was in Penny's room, putting the last stitch in his Halloween costume.

"May I put it on now?" asked Penny. "Patsy's

going to put hers on. Then she's coming right over. Won't Patsy be surprised when she sees me?"

"Maybe you will be surprised when you see Patsy," said Mother.

"That's what Patsy thinks," replied Penny. "But I know what Patsy is going to wear. She's going to be the Queen of Hearts."

"Is that so?" said Mother.

"Yepper. I saw her dress hanging in her closet. And she's going to wear a gold crown," said Penny. "Do you know how I know she's going to wear a gold crown, Mother?"

"How do you know?" asked Mother.

"'Cause it fell off the hook and hit me on the head."

"And what were you doing in Patsy's closet?" asked Mother.

"Oh, I wasn't snooping, Mother. Patsy sent me to the closet to get a game," replied Penny.

"I see," said Mother. "So Patsy is going to be the Queen of Hearts!"

"Yep!" said Penny. "Patsy's going to be the Queen of Hearts. 'Course I'm going to make believe that I'm surprised. Look, Mummy. I'll look like this when I open the door."

Penny threw up his hands and opened his eyes very wide. "Do I look surprised, Mummy?" he asked. "Do I look very surprised?"

"Oh, my, yes!" replied Mother. "You look very much surprised."

Penny laughed and turned a somersault. "It's a big joke, isn't it?" he chuckled.

Mother laughed. "It certainly is," she said.

Penny chuckled as he got undressed. He was enjoying the joke on Patsy.

After he had his bath he put on his costume. Mother held it for him. First he put one leg in, then the other leg. Then he poked his arms through the sleeves. Mother helped him to put his head into the right place. Now he could see out of the holes of the eyes. Finally Mother pulled the zipper up the back and Penny was dressed in his Halloween costume.

Penny ran to look at himself in the long mirror. He let out a whoop. There in the mirror, looking back at him, was the perfect image of Chocolate. There was the furry brown body, the big round ears, and the hard nose that now looked like a great big acorn.

Penny danced up and down with glee. "Why, I look just like Chocolate!" he cried. "I look 'zactly like Chocolate! Oh, just wait until Patsy sees me!"

Just then the doorbell rang. "There's Patsy now!" cried Penny. "I'll go down and let her in. She's gonna be surprised all right!"

Penny ran down the stairs. He swung open the front door. Then he almost fell over backwards. What he saw made him gasp. For a moment he thought perhaps he was back in the bedroom looking in the big mirror; for there stood another Chocolate, exactly like himself.

Then Penny put out his hand and touched the brown bear. "Who are you?" he gasped.

"Why—why—I'm Patsy!" came from the bear. "I didn't know that you were going to be Chocolate, too."

"I thought you were going to be the Queen of Hearts," said Penny. "I saw the dress in your closet. And a gold crown."

"Oh!" replied Patsy. "That's Mommy's dress. She's going to a party tomorrow night."

"Mother!" shouted Penny, as the two bears climbed the stairs. "Look at Patsy! She's dressed like Chocolate, too."

When the two bears came into the room, Penny's mother laughed and laughed. She

55

laughed until the tears ran down her cheeks. "Why, I can't tell you apart," she said.

"Mother, did you know that Patsy was going to be Chocolate?" asked Penny.

"Yes, I did," replied Mother. "Patsy's mother and I thought it would be such fun for you to surprise each other. We made your costumes together, so that they would be exactly alike."

Just then Patsy's mother came in. When she saw the two bears she laughed just as hard as Penny's mother had laughed.

Penny and Patsy were both feeling a little bit disappointed because each one had expected to be the only Chocolate at the party.

"Why, I can't tell which is which," laughed Patsy's mother. "Even their voices sound exactly alike, inside of those heads."

"You will have a wonderful time at the party," said Penny's mother. "Everyone will get you mixed up. Think what fun it will be to fool them."

This made the children feel much better. They began running in and out of the room to see if their mothers could tell them apart.

Then they went downstairs to the kitchen. There they had a merry time, fooling Minnie.

When it was time to go to the party, Patsy said, "I'm glad now that we are both dressed like Chocolate. We're going to have fun, fooling everybody at the party."

"We're going to fool 'em, all right," said Penny. "We're going to fool everybody."

"It's a big joke, isn't it?" said Patsy.

"Yes," chuckled Penny. "I think it's the biggest joke that ever was!"

6

More Surprises

When it was time to go to the Halloween party, Penny and Patsy asked if they could go by themselves. It wasn't very far, so their mothers agreed that they could walk over alone.

"But we will come for you," said Penny's mother. "We will be there at nine o'clock."

"Okay!" said Penny, as the two bears went out of the door.

They trotted down the street and their mothers watched them until the children turned the corner. They couldn't tell which was Penny and which was Patsy.

As the children turned the corner, they came upon Mike, a great big police dog. Mike belonged to Mr. Turner, a friend of Penny's daddy. Penny and Patsy both loved Mike and Mike was very fond of the children. But Mike didn't know the children at all, now that they were dressed like bears. To him they were just strange animals that he had never seen before. And Mike didn't like strange animals. He let out a low growl.

Penny and Patsy stood still. "Hello, Mike," said Penny. But it didn't sound at all like Penny's voice.

Mike was sure he didn't like the strange animals now, so he gave a terrific bark.

"He doesn't know us," said Patsy. "Let's run home."

"No," said Penny. "He'll run after us and he might catch us. Daddy always says you mustn't act scared."

The two bears huddled together against a stone wall. They were both trembling.

"But I *am* scared," said Patsy, beginning to cry.

Mike was barking furiously now.

"I'll take off my head," said Penny. "Then he'll see who I am. Here, Patsy, you undo the zipper."

Patsy undid the zipper and Penny took off the bear's head.

"See, Mike! It's Penny."

Mike kept his eyes on the head in Penny's hands and went right on barking.

"I want to go home," cried Patsy.

Penny laid the bear's head down on the stone wall. Then Mike came up to Penny as he always had, wagging his tail.

Penny patted Mike on the head. "See," said Penny, "he was scared of the bear's head."

Then Mike turned on Patsy and began barking as hard as ever.

"Oh, Penny!" cried Patsy. "Pull my zipper, quick. I'll take off my head, too."

Penny pulled Patsy's zipper and Patsy took off her head. But Mike wouldn't stop barking until Patsy put her head on the stone wall beside Penny's.

Then Mike stopped barking and began to wag his tail. He sniffed at Patsy and she put out her hand and patted his head.

"See, Mike, it's just Patsy," said Penny.

"Now we better hurry," said Penny, "or we'll be late for the party."

Penny reached out for the bear's head. As he did so, Mike let out a low growl. Penny drew back his hand.

Mike began to growl and bark at the two heads sitting on the wall.

"Oh, dear!" said Patsy. "Now he won't let us have our heads. We'll never get to the party."

"Let's get Mr. Turner," said Penny.

The two children went up to Mr. Turner's front door and rang the bell. In a moment, Mr. Turner opened the door.

"Well! Well!" said Mr. Turner, when he saw Penny and Patsy. "What are you supposed to be?"

"We're both Chocolate," said Penny.

"Chocolates!" exclaimed Mr. Turner. "What kind of chocolates? Sweet chocolates or bitter chocolates?"

"Bears!" said Patsy.

"Bears!" exclaimed Mr. Turner.

"Mike's got our heads," said Penny.

"Mike's got your heads!" exclaimed Mr. Turner.

"Yes, he won't let us pick them up," said Patsy. "And we're going to be late for the party."

Mr. Turner didn't quite know what the children were talking about, but he went with them to the stone wall. There was Mike, barking and snarling at the bear heads.

Mr. Turner took Mike by the collar. "Lay off those heads," he said. Then he led Mike into the house and closed the door on him.

When Mr. Turner returned, the children had put on their heads and fastened each other's zipper. When Mr. Turner saw them, he laughed very hard.

"Well, that beats everything!" he shouted. "Why, I don't know which is Patsy and which is Penny! You look exactly alike. I declare, you could fool your own mothers."

The children started for Tommy's house at a run. When they arrived, the door was opened by Humpty Dumpty. When he saw the two bears, he laughed until he shook up and down.

Humpty Dumpty led them down some stairs to a big cellar playroom. It was very gay with strips of orange paper. Big orange balloons, painted to look like jack-o'-lanterns, bobbed against the ceiling.

Eight or ten children were sitting as quiet as mice on the floor. They were all dressed in gay costumes and wearing false faces.

The two bears sat down beside each other. Next to Penny sat a very tiny old witch. She had a broom and held a toy black cat in her lap. Next to the witch was Red Riding Hood. Beside her was someone dressed like the wolf and wearing a false face with a very long snout.

On the opposite side of the room sat Little Bo Peep and a cowboy, a fairy, and a clown.

Over in a corner, all alone, sat Bluebeard. His beard was so long it touched the floor.

Then the doorbell rang and Humpty Dumpty left the room.

He returned with a little boy carrying a candle. As soon as he got in the room, he put the candle down on the floor and jumped over it. Then all of the children knew that he was

> "Jack be nimble, Jack be quick,
> Jack jump over the candlestick."

Jack sat down beside the two bears.

Then Humpty Dumpty said, "Now we will guess who everyone is."

As soon as he said this, Penny knew that Humpty Dumpty was Tommy's daddy. He could tell from his voice.

It was great fun, guessing who each child was. As each one became known, he took off his mask. There was a great deal of laughing and shouting.

Finally everyone was known but the two bears. And how Penny and Patsy giggled inside of their bear heads.

"I think they are Patsy and Penny," said Sally Andrews, the old witch.

"I'm sure they are," said Tommy. "But I don't know which is Penny and which is Patsy."

"Make them each say something," said Robert

Jameson, the cowboy. "We can tell them by their voices."

"All right," said Mr. Robbins. "Say 'I'm a little brown bear.'"

Penny and Patsy each said "I'm a little brown bear." But they sounded exactly alike. All of the children screamed with laughter.

Mr. Robbins said they would have to give it up. So the bears took off their heads and Penny and Patsy each received a prize for the best Halloween costume.

The evening passed very quickly. The children bobbed for apples in a big tub and played several games. Then they all sat down on the floor and had ice cream and pretzels.

Just as Penny finished his ice cream, he had an idea. He rushed over to Patsy and whispered something in her ear. Patsy giggled. "Oh, yes! Let's!" she said. "That will be fun!"

"What will be fun?" asked Sally, who was standing near.

"Oh, it's a secret," said Patsy.

"It isn't polite to have secrets at a party," said Sally.

"It isn't a secret about you," Patsy said. "It's something about our mothers."

When Patsy's mother and Penny's mother

arrived, the two little bears had their heads on again. They said good-bye to Tommy and his mother and father and thanked them for the lovely party. Then they trotted home beside their mothers.

The children did a great deal of giggling and whispering on the way.

"You certainly are full of giggles," said Penny's mother.

"I still don't know which is which," said Patsy's mother. "I just hope I get the right little bear tonight."

There were more giggles from the bears.

When they reached Penny's house, his mother said, "Say good night to Patsy."

The children called "Good night" and went in their houses. They were both still giggling.

"Run right upstairs now, Penny," said his mother. "It is late. I'll help you out of your costume."

When they reached Penny's room, his mother sat down on the edge of his bed. She pulled the zipper and lifted the bear's head. There, to her great surprise, was Patsy!

By this time Patsy was laughing so hard she fell right over on the bed. She laughed and laughed.

Penny's mother laughed, too. "Well, that was a surprise!" she said. "I wonder whether your mother has found out that she has the wrong bear."

In a few moments Patsy's mother came in with Penny. They were laughing, too. "I would like to exchange this little bear," she said.

The two children rolled on the bed, laughing. "Oh, boy!" cried Penny. "Have we had fun! We fooled everybody!"

"Yes," shrieked Patsy, "we fooled everybody! And didn't we scare Mike! Oh, boy! Wasn't he scared!"

7

Penny Earns Some Pennies

One day, shortly before Christmas, Penny and his mother were shopping. Penny loved to go shopping with Mother, especially when she was buying Christmas presents.

As they were walking home they passed a jewelry shop. Penny and his mother stopped to look in the brightly lighted window.

"Let's play Choose," said Penny.

"All right, let's," replied Mother.

Penny and Mother often played Choose when they looked in a shop window. "Choose" meant that they looked over everything very carefully and each chose the one thing in the window he liked best. Then each had to guess what it was the other had chosen.

Penny stood on his toes with his nose pressed against the windowpane. He looked over everything very carefully. Then he said, "I'm ready. Are you, Mummy?"

"Yes," replied Mother. "I'm ready, too."

"You guess first," said Penny.

"Very well," said Mother. "Is it a watch?"

"No, it isn't a watch," replied Penny.

"Is it a ring?" Mother asked.

"No, it isn't a ring," said Penny.

"Is it one of those pins?" asked Mother.

"No," laughed Penny. "But you're getting warm. It's near the pins."

"Oh, I know what it is," said Mother. "It's the silver rooster saltshaker."

"Yes," cried Penny, laughing. "Now I'll guess yours."

"All right," said Mother. "Fire away!"

"Is it a watch?" asked Penny.

"Yes, it is," laughed Mother. "My, but you're quick!"

Penny grinned. He looked over all of the watches. "I'm going to pick the right one the first time," he said.

"Well, go ahead," said Mother.

"Is it the one in the middle? The one that you pin on your dress?" asked Penny.

"Why, yes!" exclaimed Mother. "That's the very one!"

"I told you I'd guess it the first time," said Penny as they walked away from the window. "Would you like to have it for Christmas, Mother?"

"It would be very nice," said Mother.

"Well, maybe I'll buy it for you," said Penny.

Mother laughed. "I'm afraid you would find it too expensive, dear," she said.

"Would it cost a great deal?" asked Penny.

"I'm afraid so," replied Mother.

"More than a whole dollar?" asked Penny.

"Oh, my, yes!" said Mother.

"Maybe I could earn the money and buy it for you," said Penny.

Mother squeezed her little boy's hand and said,

"Thank you, Penny, for wanting to buy it for me. That means more to me than the watch."

"But you would like to have the watch, too, wouldn't you?" asked Penny.

"Of course, darling," Mother replied. "And someday, when you are a great big man like Daddy, you can buy one for me."

The next day Penny was watching some of the older boys play ball. Penny wished that they would ask him to play but they didn't. One boy about eight, whom they called Peter, was the best ballplayer of the group. When the game was over, one of the boys called out, "Hey, Peter! Can you come over to my house tomorrow after school? I want to show you my new catcher's mitt."

"I can't," replied Peter. "I have to deliver my newspapers after school."

"Oh, what do you want to deliver newspapers for?" said the boy.

"To earn money," replied Peter. "I have to earn money to buy a catcher's mitt."

Just then the bell rang and all of the children ran into school.

That night, after Penny went to bed, he

thought of Peter's remark about newspapers and earning money. He wondered whether he could earn some money selling newspapers. Then he could buy the watch for Mother. While he was thinking about selling newspapers he fell asleep.

The next morning he saw Peter in the school yard. Penny went up to Peter and said, "I'd like to sell newspapers."

"You're pretty little," said Peter.

"Well, I could do it," said Penny. "I know I could."

"I think you're too little," said Peter, sitting down on the school steps.

Penny sat right down beside him. "I want to buy my mother a Christmas present," said Penny.

"Oh," said Peter.

"Do you think I could sell 'em?" said Penny.

"Well," replied Peter, "I know a good corner where nobody sells 'em."

"Do you have a corner?" asked Penny.

"No, I don't have a corner," replied Peter. "I just take my papers in my express wagon and deliver them to my customers."

"Gee!" said Penny. "Do you have customers?"

"Oh, sure!" said Peter. "I have a lot of customers."

"Do you make a lot of money?" asked Penny, his eyes growing very big.

"I do pretty good," said Peter, "counting the presents I get from my customers at Christmas."

Penny's eyes grew even bigger. "You get presents from your customers!" he exclaimed.

"Yep!" said Peter.

Just then the bell rang and the two boys parted.

That night Penny dreamed that he had hundreds of customers and that they were all giving him watches. He had great piles of watches. He was shoveling them into an express wagon when he woke up.

The next day Penny watched for Peter in the school yard. At last he saw him. He went up to Peter and said, "Peter, where is the corner where I could sell newspapers?"

"Well, if you really want to," said Peter, "I'll take you over. When do you want to start?"

"Oh, I can start today," said Penny.

"Okay!" said Peter. "I'll meet you at the front door right after school."

"Okay!" said Penny.

"Don't be late," Peter called after Penny.

Penny could hardly wait for school to be over. At last the bell rang. Penny was the first one out of the door.

Patsy called after him, "Hey, Penny! Wait for me." But Penny didn't even hear her.

He reached the front door of the school just as Peter arrived.

"Come on," said Peter. "We have to get our papers first. How much money have you?"

"Money?" said Penny. "I haven't any money. I'm going to get some, selling papers."

Peter stood stock-still. "Well, you have to buy the papers before you can sell them," he said.

"You have to buy them!" exclaimed Penny, looking very puzzled.

"Sure!" said Peter. "They don't give them to you. You buy them for two cents apiece and sell them for three cents. That way you make a cent on each sale."

"Oh!" said Penny. "Well, I guess I can't sell any, 'cause I haven't any money to buy the papers."

"Well," said Peter, "tell you what we'll do. I'll buy you twelve papers. That will be twenty-four cents. Then, after you sell 'em, you can give me back the twenty-four cents. Okay?"

"Okay," said Penny.

The boys hurried along. Soon they came to a little store. Outside of the store stood a crowd of boys. They were mostly big boys. Just as Peter and Penny joined the group a newspaper truck stopped in front of the crowd. The boys rushed up to the truck.

Peter ran into the store and brought out his express wagon. "I park it here," he said to Penny.

There was a great deal of shouting and laughing as the man on the truck handed the big bundles of newspapers to the boys.

When Peter stepped up to the truck, he said, "Twelve extra tonight."

"Hello, Peter!" said the man. "Who's the little shaver with you?"

"He's a friend of mine," said Peter.

"He's not going to sell, is he?" said the man.

"Sure!" replied Peter.

"Why, that baby can't make change," said the man.

"I'm gonna teach him," said Peter.

The man laughed as he threw the pile of papers into Peter's wagon.

"Come on," said Peter, turning to Penny.

Penny trotted along beside Peter. He had no idea where he was. It was like being in a strange city. They walked several blocks to a corner where a streetcar stopped. "Now, this is the corner," said Peter. "You ought to make out pretty good here."

Peter poked the twelve papers under Penny's arm. "Now," said Peter, "I'll show you how to make change."

Penny looked at Peter with big round eyes.

"If a man gives you a nickel," said Peter, "give him two cents back."

"Oh!" said Penny.

"And if he gives you a dime, you give him a nickel and two cents back."

"Uh-huh!" said Penny.

"If he gives you a quarter . . ." Peter continued.

"What's a quarter?" asked Penny.

"Don't you know what a quarter is?" asked Peter in surprise.

Penny shook his head. Peter looked at him helplessly. At last he said, "Well, if he gives you a quarter, tell him he'll have to buy it somewhere else; you haven't any change. I gotta hurry now."

In a moment Peter had disappeared.

Penny was all alone now, standing on the corner. He held tightly to his newspapers. He felt that he had been holding them for hours before a man finally came up to him and held out three pennies.

Penny was so pleased that his face got pink and his ears pinker. "Oh, thanks!" he said, as he handed the man the paper.

"You're a little tyke to be selling papers," said the man, patting Penny on the head.

"I'm going to buy my mother a Christmas present," said Penny.

"You are?" said the man. "That being the case I'll buy two papers."

Penny thought this was wonderful. He handed the man another paper and pocketed the three cents. "Thank you," said Penny, grinning from ear to ear.

In a few moments another man came up to Penny. He, too, handed him three cents. Penny gave him a paper and said, "I'm going to buy my mother a Christmas present."

Penny guessed that the man didn't hear him because he walked off without a word.

It was a long time before anyone else came. The newspapers began to feel heavy. Penny shifted them from one arm to the other. It was beginning to get dark. Soon the streetlamps were turned on. Penny began to wonder whether he was ever going to sell another paper.

After a while a man came up to him. He handed Penny a nickel. Penny tried to think what Peter had told him about a nickel. He knew he had to give the man something, so he handed him a penny. As he did so, Penny said, "I'm going to buy a Christmas present for Mother."

"Is that so?" said the man. "Well, that doesn't make a newspaper cost four cents. Where is my other penny?"

Penny reached into his pocket and handed over the other penny.

More and more people were getting off the

streetcars now, but no one seemed to want a paper. Penny waited and waited and waited. He grew tired of standing and tired of holding his papers. Every once in a while he rattled the money in his pocket. It made him feel better.

At last a lady stopped in front of him. She opened her bag and fumbled around inside. Then she handed Penny a large coin. Penny didn't know what it was but he knew that it wasn't a nickel or a dime. So he looked up and said in a sad voice, "I haven't any change."

The lady put the coin back in her bag and walked on.

Penny counted his papers. There were eight. They seemed like eight hundred to Penny.

Suddenly Penny felt lost. He had no idea where he was and he had no idea how to get home. All he could do was stand still and hold his papers. He felt a big lump in his throat and tears smarted his eyes. Oh, how he wished that he was home!

And then, out of the legs of the crowd, Peter appeared. Peter with his express wagon. "How are you doing?" asked Peter.

"All right," said Penny, blinking back the tears.

"How many have you got left?" Peter asked.

"Eight," said Penny.

"Eight!" exclaimed Peter. "Say, you should have sold out long ago! Here, give me some of them."

Peter took six of the papers. He spoke to the men who passed. "Paper, sir?" he would say. "Evening paper, Mister?"

Penny watched Peter, openmouthed. In no time at all Peter had sold the six papers. "See, that's the way to do it," he said. "You gotta call 'em out."

Penny went up to the next group of people and called out, "Paper, Mister? Paper?"

In a few minutes he had only one left.

"Now you're doing good," said Peter.

Penny felt quite excited with only one paper left to sell. He ran up to a tall man and called out, "Paper, sir? Evening paper?"

The man stopped and looked down. "Penny!" he cried. "Penny! What are you doing!"

"Why, Daddy!" cried Penny. "I'm selling papers, Daddy."

Daddy stooped down. "Penny," he said, "Mother and I have looked everywhere for you.

Why did you do this, dear? We thought you were lost."

"I've been earning money, Daddy," said Penny. "I'm going to buy Mother a watch for Christmas."

"Goodness gracious!" said Daddy. "How did you get the papers?"

"Peter bought them for me," said Penny, as Peter came up.

"Well, Peter, that was nice of you to help Penny out. How much does he owe you for them?"

"Twenty-four cents," replied Peter.

"Let's see what you have in your pocket, Penny," said Daddy.

Penny pulled all of the change out of his pocket. "It's a lot, isn't it, Daddy?" he said.

"Well, it won't be so much when you pay Peter back," said Daddy, as he picked out twenty-four cents and handed it to Peter.

Penny looked a little crestfallen. "All that, Daddy?" he said.

"Yes," said Daddy, "the rest is yours."

"Is it enough to buy the watch for Mother?" asked Penny.

"Well, no," answered Daddy, "but maybe we

can buy it for her together. Come along now. We must hurry home. Mother is still looking for you."

On Christmas morning under the tree there was a pile of packages for Mother. Right on top was a small package. Penny stood by his tall daddy and watched her as she opened it. When she lifted the lid of the box, there was the watch that she had chosen in the jeweler's window. There was a card inside of the box. The card said, "Christmas love to Mother from her two working men."

8

Overall Trouble

Penny's home was right on the edge of a park. There was a stream that flowed through the park where Penny and Patsy went wading in the summertime. Across the stream and just beyond the park, there was a meadow where wildflowers grew.

One warm Saturday morning Penny and Patsy decided to go to the meadow and gather buttercups.

"Maybe we could take our lunch and have a picnic," said Patsy.

"Oh, yes! Let's!" cried Penny.

The children went off to ask their mothers if they could take a picnic lunch over to the meadow.

Penny's mother said that he could go. "But you must wear your old overalls," she said.

"Aren't you ever going to buy me any new overalls?" asked Penny, as he put them on.

"Oh, yes," replied Mother. "I'll get you some new ones when those are worn out."

Just then Patsy came in. She was wearing overalls, too. "My mommy says I can go," she said. "My lunch is packed in this basket." Patsy held up a little straw basket.

Soon Penny had a basket packed with lunch, and the children started off.

"Don't go beyond the new houses on the other side of the meadow," Penny's mother called after him. "And when you hear the church clock strike two, come home."

"All right, Mother," said Penny.

Soon the children reached the park. They went down by the stream. The water was clear and shallow. It gurgled over the pebbles and around the smooth stones. There was one place where the children always crossed the stream. The stones were just close enough so that they could step from one to the other. The children followed the stream until they came to this place. Penny led the way. Patsy followed, one stone behind him.

In the middle of the stream Penny stopped. There was a little piece of wood caught in a nearby rock. "Oh, look! There's a boat going down the stream," said Penny, pointing to the piece of wood. "And the whole crew will be shipwrecked against that rock unless I save them. And all the precious cargo of gold and spices will be lost."

"And precious jewels," cried Patsy. "Here's a stick."

Patsy stooped down to take a long stick from the water. As she reached for the stick, her foot slipped off the rock and down she sat, right in the stream.

In a moment Patsy had scrambled up. The seat of her overalls was very wet.

"Hey, you ought to be careful," said Penny, reaching toward the boat with the cargo of gold, spices, and precious jewels. As he stretched his arm out, his penknife fell out of his pocket.

"Oh, there goes my penknife!" shouted Penny.

Penny quickly took off his shoes and stepped into the stream. He could see his knife lying on the bottom of the stream among the pebbles. He stooped down and picked it up. But his foot slipped and with a splash Penny sat down in the stream, too.

"You ought to be careful," laughed Patsy.

Penny laughed as he got up. "Now my overalls are wet, too," he said. "But I'm glad I didn't lose my knife."

Penny decided that now that he was in the

water he might as well wade over to the boat with the precious cargo. He picked up the piece of wood and placed it in the current of the stream. He put a leaf on it and away it went, down the stream to be caught by another rock.

When Penny and Patsy reached the other side of the stream, Patsy said, "My overalls are awful wet. They stick to me."

"So do mine," said Penny.

"Maybe if we go up to that big rock in the sun and lie on our tummies, our pants will dry," said Patsy.

"Okay!" said Penny.

The children climbed up the side of the little ravine to the big rock.

"Say, it's hot!" said Penny, putting his hand on it.

"We ought to get dry pretty quick," said Patsy.

The two children lay down flat on their stomachs. The hot sun shone down on their wet overalls.

"I'm going to eat some of my lunch," said Penny.

"So'm I," said Patsy.

The children opened their baskets and began munching sandwiches.

"I'm going to save some of mine for after while," said Patsy.

"So'm I," said Penny.

When Penny finished his sandwich, he put his head down on his arm. Patsy did the same. The hot sun felt soothing on their backs. Soon they were both fast asleep. They slept soundly for a long time.

Suddenly Patsy was awakened by screams from Penny. She rolled over and looked up. There was Penny, dancing up and down. He was screaming, "O-o-o-o-o-o-o-o-o," and slapping his leg.

"What's the matter?" cried Patsy, sitting up.

"Something's up my pants! Something's up my pants!" screamed Penny.

Just then a bee flew out of the bottom of Penny's trouser leg. "It was that bee," he said.

"Did it hurt you?" said Patsy.

"No, it didn't hurt," answered Penny. "But it tickled something fierce. Come on, let's get over to the meadow. I'm all dry."

"I'm dry, too," said Patsy.

The children got down off the big rock and went over to the meadow. The meadow was yellow with buttercups. The children set to work picking them. Soon they both had a big bunch. As they picked the flowers, they got nearer and nearer to the far edge of the meadow.

Before very long they had reached the new houses that were being built on the edge of the meadow. The workmen had gone for the day. The children walked around, picking up curls of wood that the carpenter had left. Soon they came upon a big barrel.

"Oh, look!" cried Penny. "Look at the smooth, shiny black stuff in this barrel."

"Oh," said Patsy, feeling the top of the barrel. "I wonder what that is."

"I'm hungry," said Penny. "I'm going to sit on the top of this barrel and finish my lunch."

Penny put his buttercups on the ground and climbed up on the top of the barrel. He sat down.

"I want to sit on the barrel, too," said Patsy.

"There isn't any room for you," said Penny. "You sit on that box."

Patsy sat down on the box. The children ate the rest of their sandwiches while the hot sun beat down upon them. Penny kicked his feet against the barrel.

When the children finished their sandwiches, Patsy went back to picking buttercups. Penny

sat on the barrel, cutting a piece of wood with his penknife.

After some time, Penny heard the church clock strike, *Bong! Bong!*

"It's two o'clock," he shouted. "We have to go home."

"All right," shouted Patsy. "Come on."

Penny started to get up but to his surprise he found that he couldn't get up. He tried again but his overalls were stuck fast. He pulled a little harder but he felt the barrel begin to tip over. He didn't want to upset the barrel and be underneath it when it went over. The barrel was very, very heavy.

"Hey! Patsy!" he cried.

"Come on," Patsy called back.

"Patsy!" cried Penny. "Pat-t-t-s-e-e-e!"

Patsy was halfway across the meadow. She turned around. "Come on," she cried.

Penny wriggled, trying to get free. The barrel almost upset again.

"Patsy!" he shouted. "Come here!" Penny waved his arms in the air.

"What's the matter?" shouted Patsy.

"I'm stuck," yelled Penny.

"What did you say?" shouted Patsy.

"Come here," shrieked Penny, ready to cry. For Patsy was walking farther and farther away from him. "Come back," he shrieked, kicking his heels against the barrel.

Then, to Penny's great relief, he saw Patsy turn back. When she reached him, she said, "What's the matter with you?"

"I'm stuck," said Penny.

Patsy took hold of one of Penny's arms and tried to pull him off the barrel, but she almost pulled the barrel over.

"Don't upset the barrel," cried Penny.

"Well, how are you going to get off?" asked Patsy.

"I don't know," said Penny. There were tears in his eyes.

"Shall I run home and get your daddy?" asked Patsy.

"Yes," said Penny. "Get him, quick."

Patsy started off as fast as her legs could carry her. Soon she was halfway across the meadow. Then she disappeared between the trees. It was only about ten minutes before Penny saw his daddy coming across the meadow with Patsy. But it seemed a much longer time to Penny.

When Daddy reached him, he laughed. "Well,

young fellow, no wonder you're stuck. You picked an awfully hot day to sit on a barrel of pitch."

Daddy tried to lift Penny off, but he was stuck very tight.

"Well, I don't see anything to do, Penny, but to get you out of those overalls," said Daddy.

"But, Daddy, I can't go home without my overalls," said Penny.

"I'll put my coat around you," said Daddy, "and carry you."

Daddy unfastened the straps that held up Penny's overalls and unfastened the strap at the waist. Then, after some time, he managed to pull Penny out of them. Daddy took off his coat and put it around Penny. He lifted him up in his arms.

The empty overalls hung limp on the barrel. "Guess we'll have to leave the overalls," said Daddy. "They're all full of pitch, anyway."

"I wonder what the workmen will think, when they come back on Monday morning and find my overalls stuck in the pitch," said Penny.

"I'm glad I didn't sit on top of the barrel," said Patsy, as they crossed the meadow.

When Penny reached home, he got washed and dressed. His mother was out for the afternoon.

When she returned, Penny said, "Mummy, I'll have to have new overalls."

"I told you this morning that I would get you new overalls when the others were worn-out," said Mother.

"Well, they're worn-out, Mummy," said Penny.

"They are?" said Mother. "What happened to them?"

"Oh, they were the most awful overalls," said Penny.

"Is that so!" said Mother. "What was the matter with them?"

"Well, you see, Mother," said Penny, "those overalls were always having trouble."

"Having trouble!" said Mother. "What kind of trouble?"

"Oh, like getting wet when I slipped in the water," replied Penny.

"I see," said Mother.

"And then bees got inside of 'em," said Penny.

"Bees got inside of them!" said Mother. "Anything else?"

"Oh, yes! They were terrible when they got stuck in the pitch," said Penny.

"Oh, they got stuck in the pitch, did they?" said Mother.

"Uh-huh!" said Penny.

"And where are they now?" asked Mother.

"They're still stuck in the pitch," said Penny.

Mother looked across the table at Daddy. "Well," she said, "I can see we'll have to get you some overalls that won't do things like that."

"That's what I think," said Penny.

9

Peter the Ballplayer

One day Penny said to his mother, "Mummy, I wish I had a brother."

"Do you, Penny?" said Mother.

"Yes," said Penny. "Then I would have somebody to play with."

"You and Patsy play nicely together," said Mother.

"Oh, Patsy's all right," replied Penny. "We

have a lot of fun. But if I had a brother, he would play baseball and football with me. And we could play with my trains. Patsy never knows what to do with electric trains except watch them. And she can't throw a baseball. And you should see her catch. She can't catch at all."

"Well, Penny, Daddy and I have been talking about getting a brother for you for sometime," said Mother.

"You have!" exclaimed Penny. "And are you going to?"

"Yes, I think we will," said Mother.

"Oh, Mummy! How soon will he come?" asked Penny.

"I don't know, dear," replied Mother. "Daddy has written to the place where we found you, but they haven't any baby boys at present."

"Baby!" cried Penny. "I don't want a baby brother, Mother! A baby brother couldn't play baseball!"

"But he could when he grew bigger," said Mother.

"That would take too long," said Penny. "I want a big brother, Mummy."

"Oh, you do?" said Mother. "How big? As big as you?"

"Bigger," said Penny. "Do you know what, Mummy?"

"What?" asked Mother.

"I would like to have a brother just like Peter," said Penny.

"How old is Peter?" asked Mother.

"He's eight," replied Penny. "He's wonderful, Mummy. You ought to see Peter pitch balls. And he can bat 'em, too. Peter says he's going to be a baseball player when he grows up. He says his daddy was a baseball player a long time ago."

"Is that so?" said Mother.

"Yes," replied Penny. "Peter plays ball so good that the big boys in the fifth grade ask him to play with them. But he plays with me, too," said Penny. "Sometimes he plays with me all through recess."

"Well, Peter must be a nice boy from what you have told me about him," said Mother.

"Oh, he's swell!" said Penny. "You know what, Mummy? Next to you and Daddy, I like Peter more than anybody else."

"Well, I would certainly like to see Peter sometime," said Mother.

"You mean maybe we could 'dopt Peter, just

the way you 'dopted me?" said Penny, his eyes shining.

Mother laughed. "Good gracious, no!" she said. "You can't adopt little boys who have fathers and mothers."

"Maybe his mother and father would let us have him," said Penny.

"Oh, no, darling!" replied Mother. "Mothers and fathers don't give up their little boys. Especially when they are as nice as Peter or as nice as you. Can you imagine Daddy and me giving you up to someone else?"

Penny shook his head. "No," he said. "And I wouldn't want you to."

"Well, Peter wouldn't want his mother and daddy to give him up, either," said Mother.

"Do you suppose we can find a brother just like Peter?" asked Penny.

"No two little boys are exactly alike," said Mother, "but we will begin to look around. I am sure we will find the right brother for you."

One day Penny's daddy said, "Penny, how would you like to go with me to see a real baseball game?"

"Oh, Daddy, that would be great," said Penny.

"You mean the kind of baseball game you always listen to over the radio?"

"That's the kind," said Daddy.

"Oh, boy!" cried Penny. "Mother, did you hear that? Daddy's going to take me to a real baseball game. The kind you hear over the radio."

"How wonderful!" said Mother.

"When are we going, Daddy?" asked Penny.

"Next Saturday afternoon," replied Daddy.

The next morning at recess Peter came up to Penny. "Do you want to play ball?" he asked.

"Oh, Peter!" cried Penny. "What do you think! My daddy's going to take me to a real baseball game on Saturday. The kind you hear over the radio."

Peter's big brown eyes grew wide and a light came into them. "Oh, that's wonderful!" he said in a low voice. "That's wonderful. Someday I'm going to see a baseball game. Someday I am. A real baseball game, with uniforms and umpires and home runs and everything."

Peter and Penny went to that part of the playground where the children were allowed to play ball. They used a softball.

Peter threw it to Penny. When Penny threw it back, Peter said, "You mustn't throw it underhand, Penny. When you pitch a ball, you throw it like this." Peter threw the ball back with a swing of his arm. "See?" he said.

Penny threw it. The ball didn't go very far, but Peter said, "That's the way."

Penny felt all warm inside when Peter praised him.

Just then two ten-year-old boys from the fifth grade came along. "Come on, Peter," cried one of the boys. "Throw it here. Let's have a real game."

"I'm playing with Penny," Peter called back.

"Aw, what do you want to play with a first grade baby for?" said the boy. "He can't play ball."

"Well, I'm showing him how," said Peter, as he threw the ball back to Penny.

Penny tried again to swing his arm the way Peter did. He wanted to show those big boys that he knew how to throw a ball. But he tried so hard he fell down and the ball went up in the air and fell right beside him.

The two big boys roared with laughter. "Some ballplayer!" they screamed. "He can't

even stand up. Come on, Peter. Stop wasting your time with that baby."

Penny scrambled up. His face was bright pink and his ears were scarlet.

"I'm playing with Penny," was all Peter said. "Come on, Penny, throw it again."

When the bell rang for the children to return to their rooms, Penny said, "Thanks, Peter. I'm going to be a ballplayer when I get big, too."

"Sure," replied Peter. "We'll be on the team together. But I better be the pitcher."

That evening Penny told Daddy about his game of ball with Peter.

"He's a wonderful ballplayer, Daddy," said Penny. "He's the best ballplayer in the whole school."

"Do you think Peter would like to go with us on Saturday?" asked Daddy.

"Oh, Daddy! I know he would," cried Penny. "Can I ask him?"

"Yes. You ask him tomorrow," said Daddy. "Tell him to be here at the house by one o'clock."

The next morning Penny could hardly wait to see Peter. He reached school before anyone else. He stood right by the front door so that he would be sure to see Peter.

After a while the children began to arrive. They came by ones and twos and in bunches. Before very long Penny saw Peter coming. He was alone. Penny ran to meet him. "Peter!" he cried. "My daddy is going to take you to the ball game, too."

Peter's eyes lit up like two lamps. "He is!" he said. "Your daddy's going to take me to the ball game?"

"Yepper!" said Penny. "You have to be at our house at one o'clock."

"Gee!" said Peter. "That's the most wonderful thing that ever happened to me."

When Saturday afternoon arrived, Peter was at Penny's house long before one o'clock.

While Penny took his bath, Peter sat in Penny's little bedroom chair and talked to Penny's mother. Penny could hear his mother asking Peter about his daddy, who had been a baseball player. Peter spoke in such a low voice Penny couldn't hear what he said.

He heard Mother say something about Peter's mother. The water was running and Penny couldn't hear Peter's reply. While Penny splashed in the tub he could hear the murmur of Peter's voice. Every once in a while Penny could hear Mother say, "I see, dear."

It seemed to Penny as though someone was always telling Mother about something and Mother was always saying, "I see." When Mother said "I see," Penny always felt better and he guessed everyone else did, too.

At one o'clock Daddy started off with the two boys. Mother kissed Penny good-bye and then she kissed Peter. "My, but it is nice, Daddy, to have two little boys to kiss good-bye," she said.

"Hey! What about me?" said Daddy.

"I mean three little boys," laughed Mother, as she kissed Daddy.

Peter and Penny had the most exciting afternoon of their lives. They jumped up and down most of the time. They yelled for the home team until their throats were dry. Then Daddy bought them cold drinks. They ate rolls with hot dogs and plenty of mustard. When the home team scored a home run with all of the bases full, the two boys stood on their seats and jumped up and down until they were limp.

Finally, the home team won the game and it was time to go home. Peter looked up at Penny's daddy. "I didn't know a ball game could be so wonderful. Oh, boy! Wait until I grow up! I'm going to be the best pitcher that ever was."

"And I'm going to be on the team, too, Daddy," said Penny.

"You bet!" said Peter.

On the way home Daddy said, "Now, Peter, where do you live? We'll take you right home."

"Thank you, sir," said Peter. "I live at Trinity House."

"Is that so?" said Daddy.

"What's 'Trinity House'?" asked Penny.

"That's where you live if you don't have any father or mother," answered Peter.

Penny looked at Peter with eyes as round as dollars. "Haven't you any father or mother?" he asked.

"No," replied Peter. "Not since I was a little baby."

"I didn't have any when I was a little baby," said Penny. "But Daddy and Mother looked all over for me, and when they found me then I had a daddy and mother."

"Gee, that was swell!" said Peter.

Just then they reached the gates of the home where Peter lived. "Well, here we are!" said Daddy, turning to Peter.

Peter opened the door of the car. "Thank you very much, sir, for taking me to the game," he said.

"You are very welcome," replied Daddy. "We were glad you could go with us."

Penny looked ready to burst with excitement.

"Peter," he said, "Peter, you're going to have a daddy and mother, too."

Peter laughed and said, "Good-bye, Penny. I'll see you on Monday."

"Good-bye," called Penny, as Daddy started the car.

"Oh, Daddy!" cried Penny. "You'll be Peter's daddy, won't you?"

"Peter is a fine, dear boy," replied Daddy. "We will have to talk it all over with Mother."

"Oh, Mother! Mother!" cried Penny, when he reached home. "What do you think! Peter hasn't any mother or father. Isn't that wonderful, Mother? Now we can 'dopt him."

"I know, darling," said Mother. "Peter told me while you were taking your bath. I have been thinking about it all afternoon."

"And are you going to 'dopt him?" asked Penny, leaning close to his mother.

"We'll see," said Mother. "I will have to talk it over with Daddy."

That night, when Mother heard Penny say his prayer, she heard him say, "God bless Daddy. God bless Mummy. And God bless Peter, my really truly brother."

10

How the Sailboat Got Its Name

Penny was eating his cereal. It was the Monday after he and Peter had been to the baseball game. Over a large spoonful of cereal Penny said, "Are we going to 'dopt Peter today?"

"Well, dear," said Mother, "Daddy and I have been talking about Peter. We can't decide such an important thing in a hurry, you know. We feel that we want to know Peter better."

Penny's face began to look very long and sad. "I know him," he said.

"Now don't feel unhappy," said Mother. "Daddy and I have decided one thing. We are going to take Peter to the seashore with us for the summer."

"Oh, that's fine!" cried Penny. "Shall I tell him when I see him today?"

"Peter already knows about it," replied Mother. "Daddy went to see him yesterday. He will go with us as soon as school is over. In the meantime, Penny, don't say anything to Peter about our adopting him. Let's keep that a secret between you and Daddy and me."

"All right," said Penny. "But someday we'll tell him the secret, won't we?"

"We'll wait and see, dear," said Mother. "We'll know by the end of the summer."

A week later school was over and Penny and Peter, Daddy and Mother, Really, Truly, and Minnie, all left for the seashore.

The little town where Penny lived in the summer was on a small cove. The house stood on a rocky cliff right by the edge of the water. A flight of stone steps led down to the dock.

The year before, Daddy had bought a beautiful

new sailboat. When Daddy wasn't sailing it, the boat was tied to the dock. There it bobbed up and down like a restless pony.

For a long time the sailboat hadn't any name. Daddy and Mother and Penny all tried to think of a name for the boat but nothing sounded just right. Daddy said that the boat belonged to the three of them and so it should be named for all of them.

Daddy tried to make a name out of the first letters of each of their names but Mother said it sounded like one of the kittens sneezing.

At last Mother said that she had a name for the sailboat.

"What is it?" said Daddy and Penny together.

"The *Threeofus*," said Mother.

"Why, that's wonderful!" exclaimed Daddy. "That's exactly right. Now everyone will know that the *Threeofus* belongs to the three of us."

That very day Daddy painted the sailboat's name on her side. All of the neighbors came to look at her and said what a nice name it was.

Penny loved the *Threeofus*. Daddy taught him how to sail it. By the end of the summer Penny could handle either the tiller or the sail.

Peter had never been in a sailboat. The first

time Daddy took the two boys out for a sail, Peter said, "Gee! This is almost as wonderful as playing baseball."

Peter asked a great many questions about the boat. Daddy let Penny answer most of them. After all, Peter had taught Penny how to play baseball. Now Penny could teach Peter how to sail a boat.

Before the summer was over both Peter and Penny could sail the boat very well indeed. Daddy said that in another year the boys would be able to take the boat out all by themselves.

"I wish we could take it out alone this year," said Penny. "Just once."

As the summer drew to a close, everyone talked of the boat race. The race was to be held on Labor Day in the afternoon.

Everyone who owned a sailboat was certain that his boat would win the race. Peter and Penny and Daddy told each other that they were sure that the *Threeofus* would be the winner.

"She's the fastest little sailboat in the cove," Daddy would say.

"I wish I were big enough to sail her in the race," said Penny.

"Someday you will," said Daddy.

"You don't think we're big enough, do you?" said Peter.

"No," replied Daddy. "I'll have to do it this time."

"Well, we're going with you, aren't we?" said Penny.

Daddy didn't answer right away. Then he said, "Yes, I guess so."

"What do you mean, Daddy, by you guess so?" said Penny.

"Well, you see," said Daddy, "when you race, it is best to have just one for the crew. But I know that you both want to go, so we'll try it."

The morning of the race Peter sat on the dock, looking into the water. He was thinking. Penny and Daddy were busy with the sailboat. At last Peter came over to Daddy and said, "I'm not going in the *Threeofus* when you race her this afternoon."

"You're not?" said Daddy.

"No," said Peter. "The *Threeofus* stands a better chance to win the race if there are only two in her. And I want her to win."

Daddy threw his arm around Peter. "Peter," he said, "that's wonderful of you! Now, I'm sure she'll win."

The race was to start at three o'clock at the Yacht Club. The club was about two miles from the *Threeofus*'s dock.

After lunch Daddy said, "I'm going to drive up to Cooper's Point for some lobsters. I'll be back in plenty of time to take the boat up to the club."

Daddy went off and the boys went swimming.

After their swim they played on the dock. Three o'clock drew nearer and nearer.

"Daddy ought to be here soon," said Penny.

"Yes," said Peter. "Let's go see what time it is."

The boys were climbing the steps to the house when Penny's mother appeared on the porch.

"Peter!" she called. "Penny! Come quickly!"

The boys ran up the rest of the steps. "Where's Daddy, Mother?" Penny called.

"Daddy has a flat tire," said Mother. "He's stuck between here and Cooper's Point. He just telephoned to tell me."

"Oh, Mother! Are we going to miss the race?" cried Penny.

"Not if you and Peter can sail the boat down to the Yacht Club. Daddy will meet you there."

"All by ourselves!" exclaimed Penny.

"There is nothing else to do," said Mother. "Do you think you can do it?"

"Sure!" said Peter. "We can do it. We have to do it. The *Threeofus* is going to win the race."

The two boys started back to the dock. Penny's mother went with them. She helped them to put up the sail. When they were ready, she untied the rope that held the boat fast. As they set forth, she thought they both looked very little.

Peter's face was very serious as the wind filled the sail and the boat glided away from the dock.

He was taking the *Threeofus* to win the race. It was the most important thing he had ever done.

Meanwhile Penny's daddy had reached the Yacht Club. He stood on the dock, straining his eyes for the sight of the *Threeofus.* More and more sailboats arrived. They were like a great flock of birds, resting on the water around the Yacht Club.

Daddy looked at his watch. Quarter of three

and the *Threeofus* was nowhere to be seen. It looked as though she had lost the race before she started. Then, away off, Daddy saw a sailboat. It was the *Threeofus.* Slowly, as the minutes passed, she grew larger. At two minutes of three Penny threw the rope to Daddy. Daddy pulled the boat to the dock and jumped in. At the same time Peter jumped out. "You'll win. I know you'll win," was all he had time to say.

"Thanks, Peter! You're a trump!" Daddy called, as he sailed up to his place on the line.

Peter never took his eyes off the *Threeofus.* She seemed to skim over the water. Soon she was leading the race.

Peter was jumping up and down, yelling with all his might, when Penny and Daddy crossed the line ahead of all the others. "You've won! You've won! You've won!" he cried, as Penny and Daddy stepped out of the boat.

"Yes," said Daddy, "but we could not have won without you, Peter. So you step up and receive the prize for the *Threeofus.*"

Peter walked over to the president of the Yacht Club. The president handed Peter a beautiful silver sailboat. "The first prize," he said, "goes to the *Threeofus.*"

Peter said, "Thank you, sir," while everyone clapped.

The next morning when Penny and Peter finished their breakfast, they went out to look at the *Threeofus.* Daddy and Mother were standing by the boat. Daddy had a can of paint in one hand and a brush in the other. On the side of the boat, in fresh paint, was a new name. It was the *Fourofus.*

"What does that mean?" asked Penny.

Mother put her arm around Peter. "It means that we now have two little boys. We are going to adopt Peter."

"And the sailboat belongs to the four of us," cried Penny. "And Peter belongs to us and we belong to Peter. Oh, Mummy! I told you he did. Didn't I tell you?"

Turn the page to see more of Penny's
adventures in

Penny and Peter

where Penny's wishes really do come true.

1

Crabs, Crabs, Beautiful Crabs

Penny's father and mother had adopted Penny when he was a tiny baby. They had waited for him a long time but when they found Penny, he was exactly what they wanted. They named him William but they called him Penny because his curly hair was just the color of a brand-new copper penny.

When Penny was six years old, he started to

go to school. There he met Peter who was eight. He was the best baseball player in the school. Peter lived in a children's orphanage because he didn't have any father or mother. The two boys were so fond of each other that Penny's father and mother took Peter to the seashore with them for the summer. At the end of the summer, they decided to adopt Peter. So, when the summer vacation was over and it was time to return home, the two little boys knew that they were going to be really truly brothers.

"Really truly brothers for ever and ever," said Penny.

Mother and Daddy had decided to leave the seashore the week after Labor Day, but Daddy had to make an unexpected business trip so he had to leave the day after Labor Day.

Before he left, he put the sailboat away for the winter. Then he packed the car full of things that Mother said had to go back to town. When he finally drove off, there was nothing left for Mother and the boys to bring home on the train, along with Minnie, the cook, but one suitcase and the little traveling bag in which Really and Truly traveled. Really and Truly were

Penny's kittens but by this time they had grown into two very handsome cats.

"It's a great relief to have Daddy drive all of those things home," said Mother. "I would much rather go in the train. It is more comfortable than riding in the car with my feet in a pail and the floor mop hitting me on the head every time we turn a corner."

"Do you remember last year," asked Penny, "when Daddy stopped suddenly and the basket of tomatoes upset just as I slid off the seat?"

"I certainly do," said Mother. "And you landed right on top of those beautiful tomatoes. And was I angry!"

"And did we have tomato juice!" cried Penny. "It was all over everything, wasn't it, Mother?"

"It certainly was," said Mother. "But mostly all over you and the floor of the car."

Penny laughed as he recalled the mess he had suddenly found himself in, with all those tomatoes.

"We can laugh about it now," said Mother, "but it didn't seem very funny when it happened. This year, there will be nothing like that. We'll have a nice, quiet, peaceful trip home on the train."

"When are we leaving?" asked Peter.

"Next Monday," replied Mother. "We will go up on the two o'clock train. That will get us home before the rush hour."

Monday morning, after the boys had had their breakfast, they wandered around the house. They didn't seem to know what to do with themselves.

"Seems funny not to have the sailboat, doesn't it?" said Peter, as the boys sat on the dock swinging their feet.

"Seems 'though we ought to go out in a boat the very last day," said Penny.

"We could go out in the rowboat," said Peter.

"All right, let's!" said Penny. "And let's catch some crabs and surprise Minnie. It would be nice to take some crabs home with us. Don't you think so, Peter?"

"Yes," said Peter. "I love crabs. And we won't get any more until next summer."

"Well then, we'll have to catch a fish for bait," said Penny.

Penny ran to the garage to get their fishing tackle, while Peter hunted for a clam to use for fish bait.

In a short time, the boys were settled on the

end of the dock each with his line in the water. They were as quiet as two statues.

Then Peter began to pull his line. He didn't jerk it but pulled it in carefully.

"I've got one," he whispered to Penny.

Penny looked down into the water. Sure enough, there on the end of Peter's line was a good-sized fish. It was fighting hard but Peter knew how to handle his line and he landed the fish, flip-flapping, onto the dock.

Ten minutes later, Peter and Penny were out in the rowboat with half of the fish fastened to Penny's line and the other half fastened to Peter's. They sat motionless a long time, staring into the water.

"Don't seem to be any crabs this morning," said Penny.

"Sometimes they come along all at once," said Peter.

"I know," said Penny. "But sometimes you have to go someplace else."

"Well, let's wait a little longer," said Peter. They sat waiting.

All of a sudden, Peter picked up the net and scooped down into the water.

"Got one!" he said, as he lifted the net. "A great big one."

"Me, too!" said Penny. "Quick, Peter, get it."

Peter emptied his crab out of the net into the basket that the boys had placed in the center of the rowboat. Then he scooped up the crab that was busy nibbling away at the fish on the end of Penny's line.

Suddenly, the water around the boat was full

of crabs. Peter scooped them up, one after another, as fast as he could. In no time at all, the boys had caught about fifty crabs.

"Aren't they beauts!" cried Peter.

"They're the biggest crabs I have ever seen," said Penny.

Peter looked across the water toward the house on the cliff. Then he said, "Lunch is ready. Minnie has put the signal out."

At mealtimes, Minnie always hung an old red sweater on the clothesline. This was the signal to come home.

"Well, we made a good haul," said Penny, as Peter began pulling on the oars.

When the boat was secured to the dock, the boys lifted the basket of crabs out of the boat.

"They're lively critters, aren't they?" said Peter, watching the big green crabs.

"They sure are the biggest crabs we've caught all summer. They must all be granddaddies," said Penny.

The boys carried the basket between them to the back door.

"Look, Minnie!" cried Penny. "Look at the beautiful crabs we caught."

"Crabs!" cried Minnie. "What made you

catch crabs? What are we going to do with crabs when we're going home on the two o'clock train?" Minnie came to open the screen door to let the boys in.

"Goodness!" she cried. "All those crabs! How many have you got there?"

"About fifty," said Peter.

"Fifty crabs!" cried Minnie. "Fifty crabs, and we're going home on the two o'clock train."

"But they're beautiful crabs, Minnie," said Penny. "You never saw such beautiful crabs. Look how big they are."

"I'm looking at them," said Minnie. "But

what I want to know is what you're going to do with them."

Just then, Mother came into the kitchen.

"Look, Mother!" cried Penny. "Look at the beautiful crabs we caught."

"But what are we going to do with them?" asked Mother.

"That's just what I want to know," said Minnie.

"We can take them home with us," said Peter. "They will be all right in this basket. We can put more seaweed over them. They'll be all right in the train. And I love crabs."

"So do I," said Penny.

Minnie grunted. Then she said, "Come along. Lunch is getting cold. Never know what you boys will bring into the house."

"Well, the boys will have to carry the basket of crabs," said Mother. "In fact, they will have to take full charge of them. Minnie and I have enough to take care of."

"Okay!" said Penny. "We'll take care of them, won't we, Peter?"

"Sure!" said Peter.

Mother had the one remaining suitcase packed and Minnie had a large black leather bag and a shopping bag. In the shopping bag she had odds and ends. It was filled with half-empty packages of flour, cocoa, sugar, corn-starch, and raisins—things that Minnie would use up when they got back home. Also, into the shopping bag went Minnie's favorite gadgets, such as the can opener, knife sharpener, and apple corer. Sticking out of the bag were the long handles of the pancake turner and the soup ladle. The bag was sitting on the kitchen chair when Mother came out into the kitchen after lunch.

"Why are you taking the pancake turner and the soup ladle, Minnie? We have others at home," said Mother.

"Well, I just got awful fond of them," said Minnie. "Somehow, I think I'm going to need them. The pancake turner's nice and limber and the soup ladle's not too big."

Finally, the taxi was at the door to take them to the train.

Penny put Really and Truly into their travel-ing bag. There was a great deal of mewing as Penny placed the bag in the taxi. Then Peter and Penny carried the basket of crabs out and put it in the taxi.

"You boys are sure there is plenty of seaweed in the basket with the crabs, aren't you?" asked Mother.

"Oh! Sure, sure!" said Peter. "We put in a lot of seaweed, and the crabs are very quiet."

"Well, that's good," said Mother, as she climbed into the taxi. "Here's hoping they keep quiet!"

Minnie, with her bags, climbed in beside the taxi driver.

"I've traveled with lots of things in my day," said Minnie, "but this is the first time I've traveled with fifty crabs."

"But they're beautiful crabs, Minnie," said Penny.

"Oh, sure, sure! They're beautiful crabs," said Minnie. "I just hope they take a nice long nap on the train and don't get into trouble."

"What trouble could they get into?" asked Peter. "They're so quiet you wouldn't know they were in the basket." And then, as a shuffling sound came from the basket, Peter added, "Almost."

"Well, I just hope for the best," said Minnie. "I just hope for the best."

This made Mother laugh and she said, "Oh,

Minnie! Don't be so gloomy about the crabs. They are quite all right in the basket."

Minnie sighed. "I just hope for the best," she said.

When they reached the station, the train was rapidly filling with passengers. Mother carried the suitcase in one hand and Really and Truly in the other. The boys carried the basket of crabs between them and Minnie brought up the rear with her black bag and the shopping bag.

Carrying the basket of crabs up the steep steps of the car was not easy, but the boys managed it slowly.

Mother led the way to four vacant seats that faced each other in the center of the car. The suitcase she stowed away on the rack overhead. The bag containing Really and Truly she placed on the floor.

"Now, boys," she said, "you will have to put the basket of crabs between the seats and do the best you can with your feet and legs. After all, the crabs were your idea."

"Okay!" said Peter, as the boys reached the seat. "Put it down, Penny."

Penny dropped his end of the basket so suddenly that it startled Peter, and before you could say "Boo!" the basket of crabs had tipped over and nearly all the crabs and the seaweed lay sprawling in the aisle.

The excited crabs began scrambling in all directions. Women and children, nearby, jumped up on the seats to get out of the way of the pinching crabs. The children yelled and squealed. The aisle was blocked and people couldn't get through. When they saw the crabs scurrying around in the aisle and under the seats, they fled out of the doors of the car.

Minnie started to cry, "Goodness! Goodness!"

Peter righted the basket while Penny jumped up and down and cried, "Oh, Mummy! Oh, Mummy! Oh, Mummy!"

"Be quiet, Penny. Minnie, stop yelling and do something," said Mother. "Here, give me the pancake turner."

Mother pulled the pancake turner out of the shopping bag and went after a nearby crab. She scooped for it but it slid right off. Meanwhile, the other crabs were getting farther and farther away. Everyone in the car was either kneeling or standing on the seats and they were all watching the crabs.

"Oh, dear!" said Mother. "This will never do. Here, give me the soup ladle."

Minnie handed over the soup ladle. With the

pancake turner under the crab and the soup ladle pinning it down on top, Mother was able to lift one crab back into the basket. And then, the crabs in the basket started such a commotion as their fellow crab returned. Mother went after another.

By this time, most of the crabs had hidden under the seats. They could be heard scratching their claws on the floor.

"I think I can get them, Mother," said Peter. "I can get under the seats more easily."

Meanwhile, Minnie had gathered up the seaweed. She kept muttering over and over, "I never did trust crabs. They're just plain wicked."

The aisle was now cleared of everything but Peter and Penny, who went crawling up and down looking for crabs. Peter had the pancake turner in one hand and the soup ladle in the other. Every once in a while he would chase a crab out from under a seat, put the pancake turner under it, the soup ladle on top of it, and drop it into the basket. Many a time he dropped the crab and had to begin over again, but by the time the train had gone halfway home, all of the wandering crabs had been caught and were safely back in the basket. They had settled down under the seaweed.

Once, Penny looked down at the basket and said, "I'm glad we didn't lose the crabs, aren't you, Mummy?"

"Well," replied Mother, "it would have been better to have left them in the ocean."

"Oh, but Mother," said Penny, "they are such beautiful crabs!"

"Beautiful crabs!" muttered Minnie. "Just full of meanness, that's what. Nothing beautiful about them."

At the end of the journey, Mother asked the conductor if he would lift the basket off the train. Peter and Penny carried it safely to a taxicab.

At last they reached home and Mother and Minnie breathed a sigh of relief.

"I won't trust those crabs until I get them in the pot," said Minnie. And without taking off her hat, she put a big kettle of water on the stove.

When the water was boiling, she threw the crabs in one by one. As she did so, she muttered to herself, "Beautiful crabs! I just hope I never travel again with crabs. The most awful good-for-nothing nuisance in the world is a crab."

When they were done, Minnie laid the big fat crabs out on the kitchen table. Penny came into the kitchen. Minnie stood back and admired the crabs. Then a broad grin spread over her face. "My! Oh, my, Penny!" she said. "Aren't they beautiful crabs?"

CAROLYN HAYWOOD (1898–1990) was born in Philadelphia and began her career as an artist. She hoped to become a children's book illustrator, but at an editor's suggestion, she began writing stories about the everyday lives of children. The first of those, *"B" Is for Betsy*, was published in 1939, and more than fifty other books followed. One of America's most popular authors for children, Ms. Haywood used many of her own childhood experiences in her novels. "I write for children," she once explained, "because I feel that they need to know what is going on in their world and they can best understand it through stories."